Danica Dramatica

QUEEN ME!

To Tanner, my favorite princess!
Love, Mommy

To Kayla, for being a
rock star reader and a great storyteller!
Love, Aunt Lori

To Dahlia, my little fashionista!
Uncle Jerry

Nelson Publishing, LLC
Entertain. Educate. Empower.
P.O. Box 849
Bowie, Maryland 20718
www.nelsonpublishingbooks.com

ISBN-10: 0-9794171-2-0
ISBN-13: 978-0-9794171-2-2

Danica Dramatica
QUEEN ME!

by **Lori Nelson Lee**
illustrated by **Jerry Craft**

NP CHAPTERS AN IMPRINT OF
NELSON PUBLISHING, LLC / WASHINGTON, D.C.

CHAPTER 1
NO SMACKING

Fashionista Danica Darcy entered her fourth-grade classroom wearing a pair of white denim jeans, a long gray T-shirt with pink and silver rhinestones, and a matching white short denim jacket. She accessorized her ensemble with a white knit floppy hat cocked to the side, a pink scarf thrown around her neck, black sunglasses, and pink and gray high-top sneakers.

"Danica, please remove your hat and sunglasses and place them in your locker,"

Miss Prisock asked.

"Good morning, esteemed students of Albert Carroll Elementary School," Mrs. Brown said over the P.A. system, after the morning bell rang. "I would like to welcome you back from spring break and to remind everyone that next month is our annual Local Businesses for Books fundraising contest," Mrs. Brown added. "This afternoon, Mrs. Hattie Hawthorne of Hattie's Smoothies will visit us to explain the details for this year's contest and prizes."

Danica wrote on a small piece of paper, folded it in half and passed the note to her best friend, Sasha Sanchez. Before Sasha could open it, the evil wicked Paris

Pickett reached over and snatched it out of her hand.

"That's all for the morning announcements, but before I go, remember no hitting, pushing, kicking, shoving, smacking, tripping, pinching, wrestling, or harmful touching of any kind unless you want to spend some quality time with me, doing hard labor."

You could almost hear the joy in her voice at the thought of paper cuts forming on some poor student's hands after hours of filing papers for all the teachers at Albert Carroll.

"That includes placing bugs on unsuspecting classmates, Jimmy Coletti! Have a productive day!" she added in closing.

When Mrs. Brown was done with announcements, there was always a loud fumbling noise like when someone drops a phone.

Danica wanted to smack Paris for snatching her note, but Mrs. Brown had already added smacking to her list of no-no's.

"Class, please take out your journals. You have 10 minutes to complete your daily entry before the first period bell," Miss Prisock announced.

When Miss Prisock wasn't looking, Paris opened the note to read it. The note read:

THIS YEAR, THE PRIZE IS MINE. MY PRIDE WILL NOT ALLOW ME TO ENTER INTO THIS COMPETITION LIGHTLY, AND LOSE TO PARIS AGAIN. MY HEART IS OF A LION AND MY ANCESTORS ARE CLEARING A PATH TO VICTORY. I DECLARE VICTORY! ARE YOU WITH ME?

Paris burst out laughing.

"Paris, is there something funny that you would like to share with the class?" Miss Prisock asked.

Paris quickly crumbled up the note in her hand. "No. I'm just thinking about my journal topic," she replied in her thick Southern accent. "I've been inspired by a dramatic statement," she added with an eye-squinting smirk.

CHAPTER 2
SMOOTHIE QUEEN

That afternoon, when Miss Prisock's class entered the auditorium, Hattie Hawthorne was standing up front greeting teachers and students with Mrs. Brown at her side. After all the third-, fourth-, and fifth-grade students had arrived and were seated, Mrs. Brown quieted the auditorium and announced Mrs. Hawthorne.

"I am so thrilled to be a sponsor for this year's Local Businesses for Books contest," Mrs. Hawthorne said. "As always, all contest-related sales will be donated to the school's media center to purchase new books and computers."

The crowd cheered as she continued.

"Students will be asked to create an original smoothie recipe that my staff and your faculty will vote on. The top five recipes will be made and sold at your school's fair. The student with the most votes at the fair will be presented as the Smoothie King or Queen, and have your smoothie added to our menu in your name."

The audience continued to cheer.

"How cool would that be, to have a smoothie named after you?" Mrs. Brown interjected. "Are there any questions?"

Danica quickly rose to her feet with the confidence and poise of a pageant contestant and waved her hand at Mrs. Hawthorne.

"Hello. What is your question?" Mrs. Hawthorne asked as she pointed to Danica.

"I think I speak for everyone when I say thank you for presenting us with such a creative challenge," Danica said with one hand placed over her heart.

Paris rolled her eyes and sucked her teeth at Danica's statement. Danica continued with her question. "I would like to know if the Smoothie Queen will receive a tiara," she asked before sitting down.

With a puzzled look on her face, Mrs.

Hawthorne answered, "I guess we could arrange to have a crown for the winner."

Paris, who was sitting in front of Danica, turned and said, "They don't make tiaras big enough for your big poofy head."

"Oh my dear Paris, I am so going to enjoy trouncing you," Danica whispered back.

She could tell from the look on Paris's face that she had no idea that "trouncing" meant "defeating." *What a silly girl*, Danica thought to herself.

CHAPTER 3
THE BUS RIDE
★ ★ ★

On the ride home from school, while the other kids were playing, talking, yelling, and stressing out the bus driver, Danica sat at the front of the bus brainstorming different ideas for her smoothie recipe. Using her favorite purple-colored pen, she jotted down different ingredients for her smoothie. Sasha plopped down on the seat next to her.

"What are you doing, Dani?" Sasha inquired.

14

"I'm brainstorming," Danica answered without looking up.

Just then, they heard a loud voice coming from the back of the bus, rising above the other chatter. It was wicked Pickett reading Danica's note aloud for the whole bus to hear. Danica remained faced forward and closed her eyes tightly in embarrassment.

"Oh, God. She's reading it out loud," she whispered just loud enough for Sasha to hear. The back of the bus began to roar with laughter.

"She actually thinks that she can beat me," Paris said with a slight chuckle.

"My ancestors are clearing a path to victory?" one kid repeated in amusement.

"I declare victory?" another boy blurted. "Who are you, some ancient general fighting in a war?"

The kids continued to laugh.

Danica had heard enough. She suddenly snapped out of her silence and addressed the cackling crowd. "Laugh! Laugh, if you must! Your laughter does nothing but fuel my heart with the fire needed to surpass the negative aura facing me and move toward my victory!"

"What?" the boy responded. Even the bus driver looked a bit overwhelmed by Danica's outburst.

"You heard her!" Sasha added in her defense.

"When I'm Smoothie Queen, you will

17

all bow down to me! Especially you, Wicked Pickett," Danica said.

"Oooh," said the kids on the bus, who were now looking at Paris.

"Whatever!" Paris said, then quickly sat down to avoid further attention.

"Well, I guess now I know what the letter said," Sasha said as she and Danica resumed their private conversation.

"Well, are you with me?" Danica asked.

"Of course I am!" Sasha said, right before she and Danica slapped hands.

They both turned to look at Paris, who was busy texting on her phone and laughing with her friends. "It's on," Danica said behind pinched eyes.

CHAPTER 4
GUT INSTINCT

At the next stop, Sasha and Danica got off the bus. "Call your mom and ask her if you can come over. We have work to do," Danica demanded. Sasha took out her cell phone and called her mother.

As they entered Danica's house, they could hear her new baby brother crying. "Danica, is that you?" Mrs. Darcy yelled from the baby's room.

"Yes, mom," she replied. "Sasha and I are going to work on a school project."

"There's a snack on the kitchen counter for you when you're ready. There's enough for Sasha, too," Mrs. Darcy announced.

"Thank you!" the girls replied.

They entered the kitchen and dropped their book bags to the floor. Danica took out a pencil and piece of paper and laid them on the counter. Then she took out the blender from the cabinet and plugged it in. She walked over to the refrigerator and took out a bowl of strawberries, her mother's pineapple chunks, a bottle of chocolate syrup, some milk and eggs. She walked over to the pantry and took out a banana and a can of tangerines.

"Exactly what are we doing?" Sasha

asked.

"Testing my theory," Danica replied.

"Which is?" Sasha asked.

"That anything tastes good with chocolate syrup," Danica said proudly.

"What's the egg for?" Sasha questioned.

"For protein. My dad always adds an egg to his instant breakfast drink, because he says it adds protein," Danica answered.

"If you say so…" Sasha said. "How do we know how much stuff to put in the blender?" Sasha asked.

"Gut instinct. You gotta have a natural gut instinct when working in the kitchen. My mom and grandma never measure— they just know," Danica said.

"But we're not your mom or grandma," Sasha quipped.

"Just watch and learn," Danica said with a smile.

She quickly started to dump various amounts of all the products into the blender—including three eggs.

Once everything was in the large glass container, she placed the lid on and pressed the preset SMOOTHIE button on the blender. The noise from the kitchen alarmed her mother.

"Dani, what's going on down there?" Mrs. Darcy asked.

"Nothing!" she answered.

She hit the STOP button on the blender, grabbed two glasses from the cabinet and poured two smoothies. Sasha picked up a glass and smelled the contents.

"You ready?" Danica asked with excitement. Sasha didn't answer, she just stared at Danica.

"Let's drink up!" Danica said, and then they both started to drink.

"UUGGHH!!!" Sasha said with a sour face.

"Yeah, this is pretty awful," Danica agreed. "So much for natural gut instinct."

CHAPTER 5
SECRET INGREDIENT

★∴★∴

The next morning when Danica arrived at school, she was already thinking of new recipes to try and was anxious to get the school day over with so that she could get back to her blender experiments.

She was concentrating so much on her winning smoothie recipe that she didn't notice the other kids engaged in the latest gossip circle forming near Paris's locker.

"Alright everyone, let's get out of the hall and into the classroom," Miss Prisock

27

said to the small crowd.

Once inside the classroom, Sasha followed Danica over to the pencil sharpener.

"Did you hear about Paris?" Sasha whispered to Danica.

"What about Paris?" Danica asked.

"Her grandmother is sending her a secret ingredient from Savanna, Georgia for her smoothie," Sasha said.

"What!" Danica shouted.

"Shhhh!" Sasha begged.

"Do you know what this secret ingredient is?" Danica asked.

"She won't say, hence the secret," Sasha replied. "What are you going to do?"

"You think you could come over after

29

school again today?" Danica asked.

"I can't today. I have soccer practice," Sasha said.

Miss Prisock noticed the girls having a conversation by the pencil sharpener.

"Ladies, have a seat, please. You'll have plenty of time to chat during lunch," she ordered.

As they walked slowly to their seats, Sasha asked again, "So, what are you going to do, Dani?"

Danica shrugged her shoulders and replied sadly, "I have to come up with a winning recipe quickly, or Paris is going to walk away with my tiara."

After speaking with Sasha, Danica's mood changed from confident to uncertain. She couldn't concentrate in any of her classes, and worst than that, she was completely empty of recipe ideas.

She had no idea how she was going to defeat Paris. She thought about switching schools or even faking sick until the end of the school year, just so she wouldn't have to hear Paris gloat over her victory. A permanent visit to her grandparents' house in Orlando, Florida could work, too. The only problem with all of these crazy plans was getting her parents to go along with them.

CHAPTER 6

TELL MAMA

★:★.

Danica slowly walked through her front door, passed by the living room and into the kitchen, where she dropped her book bag to the floor before noticing her mother sitting at the table feeding her baby brother, Deon, his bottle. She sat down in the chair next to her mother and placed her head on the table.

"Dani, what's up with the slow, sad entrance? Did something happen at school today?" her mother asked.

"My clear path to victory has been smeared by Paris's grimy secret ingredient. I fear that once again she will reign supreme," Danica announced.

"What in the world are you talking about, Danica?" her mother asked, trying to hold back a small laugh at her daughter's overly emotional statement.

Danica spent the next fifteen minutes updating her mother on the contest, Paris, her lack of natural gut instinct, and the secret ingredient. Mrs. Darcy sat quietly during Danica's update, waiting for her daughter to finish. Danica always thought her mom was a good listener. When Danica finished speaking, Mrs. Darcy spoke.

"Have you done any research on how

to make a smoothie, or even looked for any recipes?" she asked.

"No," Danica replied.

"Then how do you expect to win, Danica?" her mother asked. "It sounds like you are spending too much time worrying about Paris, and not enough time properly preparing Danica."

Danica lowered her eyes. Her mother lightly lifted her chin with a gentle finger.

"Dani, the ancestors may have cleared your path, but you still need to be prepared to walk the distance," Mrs. Darcy said with a smile. She kissed Danica on the forehead and took Deon upstairs for a diaper change.

CHAPTER 7
THE GOOD STUFF

The next day at school, Danica and Sasha received permission to spend their lunch break in the media center to do research for the smoothie contest. Mr. Holland, the media teacher, was there to monitor student online activities and maintain the computer software programs.

A simple Internet search pulled up hundreds of different types of smoothie recipes; they found chocolate smoothies, peanut butter smoothies, watermelon smoothies, blueberry smoothies, orange smoothies, lemon smoothies, strawberry smoothies, banana-split smoothies… you name it, and there was a smoothie for it. With Mr. Holland's approval, they printed their top 10 recipes.

"This research is making me hungry," Sasha said.

"You just finished eating lunch," Danica replied.

"Yes, but I didn't have dessert," Sasha quickly pointed out.

As the girls organized and categorized their printouts, one particular recipe stood out as Danica's favorite: Fran's Peach Cobbler Smoothie. Peach cobbler happened to be one of Danica's favorite desserts, and she was curious to find out how it would taste coming through a straw.

"I think I found it!" Danica announced.

"Found what?" Sasha asked.

"The smoothie that will make me

queen!" she said.

That evening at home, Danica told her parents about the research she had done at school and showed them the recipe.

"What do you think?" Danica asked.

"I think I'm impressed," Mr. Darcy said.

"Sounds like you're starting to take this competition seriously," her mother added.

"Can you take me to the grocery store to pick up the ingredients?" Danica asked.

"We'll do better than that," Mr. Darcy answered. "The key to any recipe is in the ingredients. We'll take you to the farmer's market where everything is fresh and organic. Then we'll really bring this recipe to life!" he added.

That weekend, Danica put on her favorite khaki pants, her green Princess Hillary shirt, and matching purple and green sneakers. She wanted to look good while shopping.

Mr. and Mrs. Darcy, Danica and baby Deon drove out to the farmer's market where they were greeted by a rainbow assortment of brightly colored fruits and vegetables naturally grown to perfection. They took their time browsing and tasting many samples before purchasing organic milk and yogurt, fresh peaches, pure honey, vanilla extract, cinnamon sticks, and fresh nutmeg and ginger.

"Mmmm! It smells good!" Danica said after sniffing the inside of the shopping bag.

"Wait until you taste it," her mother replied.

CHAPTER 8
THE FINALISTS

Danica and her dad spent the next couple of weeks working to come up with the perfect combination of ingredients to produce the best-tasting peach cobbler smoothie ever. It was important for Danica to use the original recipe as a starting point but to enhance it to fit with her own taste. So she and her dad gave the recipe a little extra love.

The day finally came for Mrs. Hawthorne and the other judges to select their top five finalists for the smoothie contest. Danica could hardly wait to find out if she made the list. Principal Brown posted the final list outside the main office just before the lunch bell.

"Hurry!" Danica pleaded, as she and Sasha rushed to the main hall after the bell rang.

"I'm moving as fast as I can, Dani," Sasha replied.

When they reached the main office, there was already a crowd surrounding the list.

"Excuse me. Pardon me. Let's keep it moving, people!" Danica said as she and Sasha pushed their way through the crowd.

46

When they finally made it to the front, the first name that appeared on the list was PARIS PICKETT.

"Great," Danica said to herself in a disappointed tone. Her eyes continued to search down the page for her name, until she saw listed next to #4, DANICA DARCY.

"YES!" Danica and Sasha cheered while jumping up and down and hugging each other.

"Now we just have to make sure that you get more votes than Paris," Sasha said.

Danica had one week to get the word out. She needed to get as many people as she could to vote for her smoothie. She and Sasha invited everyone they knew to come support her. They invited their families, friends, coaches, pastors, community workers, and neighbors. They gave each person an orange-colored ticket to use for voting.

She didn't seem to be as concerned with the other finalists as she was with Paris. As far as she was concerned, Paris was her top competitor. Soon, Danica would go face-to-face in battle for the Smoothie Queen title.

CHAPTER 9
OH, IT'S ON!

The students, faculty, and parents had
been setting up for the school fair since
7:00 a.m. The rides were ready to go, the
games were all in place, the stage was set
up and awaiting the first show, and the food
stands were prepared to feed the expected
crowd.

A special area was reserved and
decorated for the smoothie contest. There
were five small wooden countertop booths
painted in different colors with a number

and the name of the smoothie painted in black on the front. The color of the booths matched the color of the tickets given to the students to collect votes. There were balloons surrounding the area and a large banner hanging over top that read: LOCAL BUSINESSES FOR BOOKS FUNDRAISER CONTEST SPONSORED BY HATTIE'S SMOOTHIES.

Danica and Sasha walked over to Danica's booth, where her mom had already dropped off her ingredients, blender and other tools. The booth was orange like her tickets, and on the front it read: #4 DANICA'S ORGANIC PEACH COBBLER SMOOTHIE. As she continued to look around, she saw a blue booth that read: #5 MIKE'S BLUESTBERRY SMOOTHIE; a red booth that

51

read: #3 KATIE'S STRAWBERRY MADNESS SHORTCAKE SMOOTHIE; a purple booth that read: #2 JUSTIN'S JAZZY GRAPE SMOOTHIE; and finally a brown booth that read: #1 PARIS'S COUNTRY PEACH COBBLER SMOOTHIE.

"You have got to be kidding me!" Danica yelled.

"What's wrong?" Sasha asked.

"Look at Paris's booth!" she replied in a panic.

Sasha glanced over in Paris's direction. "Unreal," Sasha said, shaking her head. "What are the chances that you and Paris would end up competing using the same flavored smoothie?"

"Apparently, extremely high," Danica answered.

Just then, Paris walked over to Danica's booth.

"I see someone told you about my recipe," Paris said.

"Nobody told me anything, Paris," Danica replied.

"No matter, I'm still going to win. You may have stolen my recipe, but you don't have my secret ingredient—authentic Southern peaches, straight from Savannah, Georgia." Paris said proudly.

"I told you, I didn't steal anything! Stealing is for people with no class or sense of fashion. I found my recipe on the Internet, and then me and my dad changed it around to make it better," Danica said defensively.

#4

**Danica's Organic
Peach Cobbler
Smoothie**

Paris began to laugh. "You think you're going to beat me with an Internet recipe?" Paris asked before turning and walking away still laughing.

"Now what?" Sasha asked.

"Now it's really on. Sound the bell and call the paramedics, cause wicked Paris Pickett is going down," Danica said.

CHAPTER 10
AND THE WINNER IS...

★ ★ ★

As people began to make their way over to the smoothie booths, Danica and Sasha did everything they could to get their attention and draw them over to their booth.

"Made with fresh ingredients from local farmers!" Danica announced.

"Made with real Georgia peaches!" Paris responded in an overly exaggerated Southern twang.

"All-natural and organic!" Danica announced.

"Free whipped cream topping!" Paris responded.

The battle went back and forth for hours. At one point, the girls even got into a singing and dancing contest to see who could attract more customers with her performance.

Customers were flocking to the smoothie booths to see what all the commotion was about, and then they purchased smoothie samples and voted using the colored tickets.

When the contest was over and votes were tallied, Principal Brown made her way to the stage to announce the winner. Danica and Paris anxiously awaited the results.

"I would like to thank everyone for making this year's fair one of our most successful," Principal Brown said. "At this time, I would like to announce the winners of the Hattie's Smoothies contest. In third place we have Katie's Strawberry Madness Shortcake," Principal Brown announced.

The crowd cheered as Katie made her

way to the stage to collect her ribbon, certificate and coupons for future smoothies. Danica glanced over at Paris, who was standing alone. She realized that she had not seen Paris's family all day. Actually, she hardly ever saw Paris with her family. For the first time, Danica actually felt sorry for her. Then Danica looked to her right and saw Sasha, Sasha's parents, her mom, her dad, and even baby Deon. Danica was surrounded by love.

"In second place we have Justin's Jazzy Grape," Principal Brown continued. Again the crowd cheered as Justin made his way to the stage to collect his prizes.

Finally, it was time to find out who

would reign as the queen and proudly wear the tiara. Just before Principal Brown made the announcement, Danica's mother turned to her and softly said, "Dani, win or lose you will always be our princess. We don't need a crown to know that."

Then Principal Brown announced, "In first place we have... we have a tie, it looks like." She looked just as surprised as the crowd. "Both winners will have their smoothies featured at Hattie's Smoothies," Principal Brown said before continuing. "Tied for first place are Paris's Country Peach Cobbler and Danica's Organic Peach Cobbler!"

"What!" Sasha yelled.

CHAPTER 11
BOW TO THE QUEEN

The crowd cheered louder than before. Paris pushed her way through the crowd, rushing to the stage to claim the tiara before Danica. Danica was busy getting hugs and kisses from her family and friends, then she finally made her way to the stage.

"Because we weren't expecting a tie, I'm afraid we have only one crown," Principal Brown said, slightly embarrassed. Paris snatched the tiara from Principal

Brown, and Danica snatched it from Paris, just before Principal Brown snatched it back.

"No snatching, remember!"
Principal Brown said, referring to her long
list of no-no's. "Mrs. Hawthorne has agreed
to give one of you $50 in place of receiving
a crown."

Danica was determined to get that
tiara. She looked over at Paris, ready to go
to battle for her tiara. As she stared at Paris,
Danica's mean, harsh expression began to
soften. Suddenly, Paris Pickett didn't look
wicked as much as she looked sad.

Danica glanced out into the crowd
and saw her family and friends waiting for
her, and then looked back at Paris. At that
moment, she realized that she didn't need
to be queen because she was already a
princess, and that was good enough for her.

She took a step back from Principal Brown and the tiara.

"I want my tiara!" Paris demanded.

Danica looked up at Principal Brown and smiled. "I'll take the $50," Danica announced. "I can use it toward taking my family and friends out to dinner to celebrate."

Paris gave her an evil smile, then said "loser."

Danica didn't respond, she simply smiled at Paris, took her prizes and exited the stage. As she walked away, Paris watched as Danica's family and friends surrounded her, showering her with more hugs and kisses. All of a sudden, winning didn't feel so great. Paris turned and exited the stage in the opposite direction. When she reached the bottom and began to walk toward the parking lot, she felt a tap on her shoulder. When she turned around, there was Danica standing in front of her.

"So, if you're not doing anything, my family and I would like for you to join us at dinner. Justin and Katie and Mike are coming too."

Paris was confused and a little suspicious.

"Yeah, Paris, Danica's paying. How can you refuse?" Sasha said smiling.

"We would love to have you," Mrs. Darcy added.

Paris smiled shyly.

"You'll have to call your mom to get

permission," Mrs. Darcy said.

Everyone started walking to the parking lot as Paris talked to her mother. She hung up the phone and caught up to Danica.

"Congratulations on winning first place," Paris said.

"Congratulations to you too, Paris," Danica replied.

"Hey, what was the name of the recipe you found online anyway?"

"Fran's Peach Cobbler Smoothie," Danica answered.

"NO WAY!" Paris shouted.

"What?" Sasha asked.

"My grandmother's name is Fran! It's short for Francine," Paris replied.

"You think…" Sasha started to ask.
"No, it couldn't be the same Fran, could
it?" she questioned.

The girls looked at each other in
silence. Then Paris, Danica and Sasha burst
into laughter.

"Well, I guess your family's secret
recipe isn't such a secret anymore," Danica
said.

"What are the chances that you two
would end up using the same secret
recipe?" Sasha asked still laughing.

"Apparently, extremely high," Danica
said.

The girls laughed all the way to the
restaurant.

Organic Peach Smoothie

by: D'Lisia E. Bergeron

Organic Ingredients:

15 oz fresh peaches cut in squares

5 scoops of organic or all-natural vanilla ice cream

2 cups whole organic milk

1/4 cup fresh squeezed orange juice

1 cup crushed ice

Put all ingredients into a blender. Mix until smooth.

Enjoy!

About the Author

Lori Nelson Lee has a passion for educating kids through creative storytelling. Her book, *Hillary's Big Business Adventure* has appeared on national and local television shows on CBN, CW, NBC, CBS, FOX, and ABC networks. In addition to writing children's books, Lori also loves writing and producing film projects, watching cooking and design shows, and traveling with her awesome husband, Tracey! Lori is a native Baltimorean and graduate of Howard University. Lori and her awesome husband reside in the Washington, D.C. Metropolitan area with their awesomely fabulous daughter.

29685883R00044

Made in the USA
Middletown, DE
28 February 2016